# Nothing Rhymes with

# ORANGE

## by Veronica Lloyd

ISBN: 978-1-989058-29-9

# Dedication

To Oaklin,
who always tries
to be a good friend.

Orange loved being orange.

He loved how round his name felt when he said it.

He loved how bright and cheery he looked.

And he especially loved all the things he could be.  Pumpkins and carrots, flowers and fall leaves.

"Being orange is wonderful!"  he said each morning.

One day, when Orange was at the park, Red said she had a new game.

"It's called rhyming!" Red bounced up and down in excitement.

"How does it work?" asked Orange.

"Say your name and then a word that sounds like it," she explained.

"Green grass!" Green shouted, eager to start playing.

"That's not a rhyme," said Red.

"They both start with 'g'," Green protested.

Red shook her head. "No, it has to sound the same at the *end*. Listen to me. Red bed, red fed, red led."

"Oh!" Green tried again. "Green seen."

"Perfect," said Red. "Blue, it's your turn."

"Blue two," grinned Blue. "Hey, this is fun!"

"Of course it is," Red said. "*My* games are *always* fun!"

After hearing what Red had said, the other colours began to create rhymes for their names.

"Pink wink."

"Brown down."

"Purple..." Purple paused and wrinkled his brow. "Umm..."

"Come on, Purple. You're holding up the game." Red crossed her arms and rolled her eyes.

Orange leaned towards Purple and whispered, "Circle."

"Purple circle!" shouted Purple.

"Hmm…" Red frowned then nodded. "Okay. It's not exactly a rhyme but I guess it's close enough. For now."

Orange smiled. Purple was his best friend and friends stuck together.

More colours joined in the game, each calling out a rhyme.

"White light."

"Black tack."

"Yellow jello," said Yellow waving his arms and shaking like a bowl of jello.

The other colours giggled and waved their arms as well.

Finally, only Orange hadn't had a turn.

"Okay Orange. What's your rhyme?" Red looked at him expectantly.

"Orange porange!" Orange laughed and so did the others.

All except Red that is. She stared at him sternly, her hands on her hips. "It has to be a *real* word."

"Why?" asked Orange.

"Because it's *my* game," said Red. "Rhyming is *not* a joke!" She picked up her sign and waved it at him.

"Sorry," said Orange. He thought hard. "Orange borange?"

"No," said Red.

"Orange forange?"

"NO!" said Red.

"Orange doesn't have a rhyme." Blue laughed and poked him. "Nothing rhymes with orange!"

"That's not true." Purple stepped closer to Orange. "Just give him time."

The colours looked at Orange waiting to hear his answer.

Orange shrugged. "I can't think of one."

Red waved her sign again. "You have until tomorrow or you can't be in the rhyming club."

As the other colours walked away, Orange looked at Purple. "There's a club?"

"I guess so." Purple gave him a friendly nudge. "Don't worry, you'll find a rhyme tonight. I know you will."

That night Orange sat in his room trying to think of a rhyme for his name.

He wrote the alphabet on a piece of paper then crossed out the vowels so the list didn't seem quite so long. After that, he began to use the consonants.

Borange, corange, dorange? No.

Forange, gorange, horange... When he got to zorange, he sighed. What was he going to do? Tomorrow, he'd be the only colour not in the rhyming club.

His stomach began to hurt as he imagined sitting alone watching the others play. Why had he ever thought being orange was so great? Being orange was awful!

He tried to make himself feel better by thinking of things that were orange. Basketballs and butterflies, balloons and orange juice... He paused as an idea suddenly popped into his head.

Could it be...? Maybe...? Of course! Why hadn't he thought of it before?

Grinning, he climbed into bed. Tomorrow he'd be in the rhyming club just like everyone else!

The next day, Red was already talking when Orange arrived at the park.

"I get to go first because this is *my* game," said Red. "*My* name has more rhymes than anyone else. Listen to this. Red sled, red bread, red shed, red Fred, red thread."

When Red finally stopped talking, the other colours shared their rhymes.

"Green screen."

"Brown clown."

"Pink think."

"Purple circle," shouted Purple. He paid no attention to Red when she grumbled it still wasn't exactly a rhyme.

At last it was Orange's turn. He took a deep breath and said...

"Orange orange!"

All the colours looked at him with puzzled expressions.

"Orange orange what?" Red put her hands on her hips.

"Just orange orange." Orange felt very clever because he was tricking the others.

Red sighed loudly. "You can't use the same *word*."

"It's not the same word." Orange explained. "I rhymed orange the colour with orange the fruit."

Everyone was silent.

Orange's grin began to fade. Maybe his brilliant idea wasn't quite so brilliant after all. In fact, he had the oddest feeling he was getting smaller and smaller the longer the others stared at him.

Blue started to snicker. Then Red began to giggle and soon all the colours were rolling on the ground laughing. All except Purple, of course, because Purple was a good friend.

"What's so funny?" Orange wrinkled his brow.

"You're not a colour, you're a food," laughed Red. "You'd better leave before we eat you!"

Orange's chin trembled. Being laughed at hurt his feelings and so did Red's words. He blinked quickly as he tried not to cry then he turned and walked away.

Purple followed Orange.

"You don't have to leave," said Orange. "I'm the one they don't want to play with.

"It wouldn't be any fun without you," Purple replied. "We're friends and friends stick together."

"It's all my fault." A tear rolled down Orange's cheek. "Nothing rhymes with orange."

"There must be at least one rhyme for you." Purple stared up at the sky and tapped his chin. "What about blorange?"

"Blorange isn't a word." Orange shook his head. "It's like saying blurple."

"Blurple is sort of fun to say." Purple grinned.

Orange sniffed and wiped away his tears. "So is blorange."

"Listen to this. Flurple, glurple," giggled Purple.

"Glorange, splorange," chuckled Orange.

"Slurple, swurple!" shouted Purple.

They both burst out laughing.

"You know," said Orange when he could finally catch his breath. "Maybe having a real rhyme isn't important after all."

"I think you're right," said Purple. "That's what makes us unique."

Orange nodded. "And silly rhymes *are* fun!"

"Do you want to get some ice cream?" asked Purple.

"Sure!" Orange nodded. "What flavour are you going to get?"

"I think I'm going to ask for... *burple!*"

Orange laughed. "And I'm going to ask for orange because..." He paused and looked at Purple, then they finished the sentence together.

"Nothing rhymes with orange!"

And as they headed for the ice cream shop, Orange smiled. Being orange really was great and so was having a good friend!

# Reading Notes

As an educator, I try to include teachable moments in each book I write. Here are a few discussion points you might want to use when reading this story with children.

1. Before reading the book, ask the children to make some predictions. Look at the character on the cover. What is he doing? How do you think he is feeling? What might the story be about?

2. Point out examples of body language in the story such as "Red crossed her arms and rolled her eyes." What is her body language telling you? Notice other examples of body language in the story.

3. The word 'my' is often in italics when Red is talking. Explain this indicates you say the word with more emphasis. What does it tell you about Red's character when she continually says the word 'my' (e.g., my game, my name, my rules)? Why do you think she acts this way?

4. When it says Orange's stomach began to hurt, ask the children if they have ever felt this way. What were they concerned about? What did they do to help deal with the feeling?

5. Pause when Orange announces he is rhyming his name with the fruit orange. Give the children time to predict how the other colours will react.

6. Discuss what the other colours could have done when Red told Orange to leave. Why might it be difficult to stand up to someone like Red?

7. How did Purple show he was a good friend throughout the story?

8. After reading the book, refer back to the section about orange the fruit and orange the colour. This can be used as an introduction to the concept of homonyms.

Thank you for reading my book. I hope you enjoyed it.
Please contact me if you have any comments or questions!

Books by this Author

Charlie
My Wrinkled Heart
Pancakes for Breakfast, Pancakes for Lunch
I See Ice Cream
The Colours of the Seasons
Nothing Rhymes with Orange

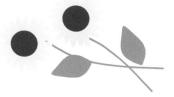

Contact Information
email: Veronica.Lloyd.Author@gmail.com
website: https://veronica-lloyd.wixsite.com/veronicalloyd

CPSIA information can be obtained
at www.ICGtesting.com
Printed in the USA
BVHW011159150223
658178BV00006B/1